Sam and the BEST DAY EVER

Dede Stockton

Sammi Jo and the BEST Day EVER

TATE PUBLISHING
AND ENTERPRISES, LLC

Published by Tate Publishing & Enterprises, LLC
127 E. Trade Center Terrace | Mustang, Oklahoma 73064 USA
1.888.361.9473 | www.tatepublishing.com

Tate Publishing is committed to excellence in the publishing industry. The company reflects the philosophy established by the founders, based on Psalm 68:11,
"The Lord gave the word and great was the company of those who published it."

Book design copyright © 2014 by Tate Publishing, LLC. All rights reserved.
Cover design by Joseph Emnace
Interior design by Gram Telen
Illustrations by Eric Gonzales

Published in the United States of America

ISBN: 978-1-63063-830-6
1. Juvenile Fiction / General
2. Juvenile Fiction / Social Issues / Friendship
14.03.05

Dedication

To the many wonderful people in my family who encouraged these adventures to begin:

My children, Cody and Kirstin, without whom this story would never have even begun.

My husband, Richard, for encouraging me to move forward on this writing adventure.

And my grandchildren, Jake and Cooper, for whom the stories continue.

Thanks to all of you!

Ten percent of all sales will be going to the Fisher House in honor of the many family members and friends that have served, are serving, and have given their lives to service of the United States of America.

Fisher House Foundation is best known for the network of comfort homes built on the grounds of major military and VA medical centers nationwide and in Europe. Fisher Houses are beautiful homes, donated to the military and Department of Veterans Affairs. These homes enable family members to be close to a loved one at the most stressful time—during the hospitalization for a combat injury, illness or disease.

You, too, can donate to this worthwhile cause at: www.fisherhouse.org.

Contents

Meet Sammi Jo

Samantha Josephine, or Sammi Jo as her friends call her, is eight years old and attends a very elite boarding school in New York City. A boarding school is a place where children live *and* go to school. She lives at a boarding school because her parents are very famous writers and they travel a lot and can't take her with them. So, during the school year, she lives at the boarding school. During the summer, she lives with her parents at their cottage on the New Hampshire shores. Her parents spend their summers writing at the cottage, so they can spend time with their only daughter, Sammi Jo.

Sammi Jo is a quiet, but well liked little girl. She has bright red hair, like her mother, blue eyes, and a just a few freckles sprinkled across her little button nose. She has a lot of friends at the boarding school, but misses her parents a lot. They come to visit whenever they are in town and then they take her and her friends out to fancy restaurants or sometimes even a play. Sammi Jo loves it when her parents come to town.

"Hey, Sammi Jo," asked her best friend, Kara, "when are your parents coming to town again?" Kara always gets to go with them, so she looks forward to Mr. and Mrs. Meriwether coming to town almost as much as Sammi Jo does.

"They probably won't be back again before school lets out," said Sammi Jo. "There are only a couple of weeks left and then they will be here to pick me up and take me to the shore! Are you sure you can't come and stay with us this summer?"

Kara usually goes with Sammi Jo and her parents for at least a few weeks out of each summer. Sammi Jo is an only child and it sometimes gets really lonely at the shore with no one else to play with.

"No," replied Kara, "I can't come this year. My parents have planned a big family vacation, so I need to spend the whole summer with my family. I'm really sorry, though. I know how lonely it will be for you. I really wish I could come."

"That's okay," sighed Sammi Jo, "I'll find something to do, I usually do."

Sammi's parents spend a lot of time writing, so Sammi would have to entertain herself while they were busy. They love Sammi Jo very much, but they also have to keep working and summertime is when they get most of their writing done, since they spent so much time travelling on book tours in the winter time. Sammi didn't mind most of the time, but without Kara there for a few weeks, it seemed like it would be a very long and boring summer.

At the boarding school, there was no time to be bored. They were all woken up at 6:00

a.m. every morning to get dressed and ready for school, and then off to breakfast. They went to class right after breakfast and stayed in class until lunch time. This was their time to spend with friends and get some time outside in the sunshine before attending their afternoon classes. After classes, they would have organized games such as: baseball, basketball, volleyball, tennis or golf until time for dinner. Then they had to do their homework and get ready for bed. There wasn't a lot of free time, so there was no time to get bored.

Sammi enjoyed the routine and being around all her friends all day. She was looking forward to being at the shore and being with her parents, but she knew that she would be very lonely. She tried to look at the bright side and think about all the adventures she might encounter at the shore, but that didn't always work. As the final days of school slid by, she began to get more and more sad. She really wished that Kara could come with them.

A Tearful Farewell

The last day of school had finally arrived. Everyone had been packing and getting ready for the last week. Classes had been cut short, so all the girls would have a chance to get packed up before their parents arrived to pick them up. Some girls had to stay there all summer for many different reasons, but there were always lots of activities planned during the summer as well. Sammi Jo felt very sad for those girls, but she didn't know any of them well enough to ask them to spend the summer with her.

After breakfast, all the girls were sent outside to await the arrival of their parents. It was like a

big party! All the girls were anxiously watching each car as it turned into the driveway, hoping that the next one would belong to their family. The air was filled with shouts of "Hi honey! We've missed you!" and laughter as one by one, the girls were packed into their family car, after hugging and saying good-bye to all their friends.

Finally, Sammi Jo's parents arrived, with Kara's parent's right behind them.

"Oh, Kara, here they come," sighed Sammi Jo mournfully.

"It will be okay!" encouraged Kara. "We can call each other and write letters to each other. Summer will be over before you know it and then we'll be right back here! Maybe you will make some new friends at the shore."

"No, our house is the only one along that side of the shore and my parents won't let me walk to the other side by myself, so unless someone happens to be walking down where we live, I'll never see another person," wailed Sammi Jo.

Both of their parents walked up right then, and Sammi Jo quickly wiped away her tears. She didn't want her parents to know how much she dreaded spending the whole summer at the shore. She didn't want them to feel sad and they would if they knew she was sad. So, she wiped off her tears and gave them a big, cheerful smile. "Hi Mommy, hi Daddy!" she cried. "I've missed you so much!"

Sammi Jo was really happy to see both of her parents, but really sad to say good-bye to Kara. She and Kara did everything together. They shared a room, they had all their classes together, they ate together, they did homework together and they loved the same sports. Sammi Jo felt like she was being pulled in two. She knew that she would see Kara again in a couple of months, but it felt like forever!

"Come on, honey, it's time to go!" said her mother, with a bright and happy smile. "I'm so excited to have you back! Let's get moving, so we can catch up and I can hear all about what's been going on with you lately."

"Bye, Kara," said Sammi Jo sadly, "it's sure gonna be lonely without you. Have a great time on your vacation! Don't forget to send me a postcard!"

"I will…and I won't," laughed Kara. She was very excited about her vacation in Europe. She knew how sad Sammi Jo was and tried not to act too excited, but it was so hard! "We'll see each other again real soon. I'll bet you will have a wonderful summer. You could meet some new friends and have some great adventures, you'll see. Please try to smile."

"Okay," said Sammi Jo, with a weak little smile, "I'll try, but I still wish you were going to be there…"

"Hop in the car, Sammi Jo!" boomed Sammi's dad, Mr. Meriwether. "We've got a lot to do before heading to the shore. Let's shake a leg," he said with a big grin on his face while standing next to the car shaking his leg.

Mr. Meriwether was a big man with a big voice who was fond of making jokes and trying to make Sammi Jo smile. He succeeded and Sammi Jo skipped over to the car and climbed in. Her dad had already packed all of her things, so with one last wave to Kara, they drove away.

Their first stop would be at their apartment in New York City before heading to the cottage.

New York Living

Sammi Jo's New York house was really an apartment. Lots of people in New York live in high-rise apartment buildings because there is very little land in the city of New York. The people who want to own actual houses live outside the city, and have to drive or take a train or a bus to work. Sammi's parents weren't around often enough to worry about having a house. Their apartment worked quite nicely for them.

Their apartment was on the top floor of the building, the penthouse. That means they had to ride the elevator to the twentieth floor. They had

a doorman who opened the door for everyone and knew everyone's name. His name was Karl.

"Welcome back, Sammi Jo!" cried Karl as he held the front door open for her. "You have grown so much I hardly recognized you."

He beamed at her as she smiled back at him. Karl said those same words to her every time he saw her. Sammi often wondered what he would say to her when she was all grown up. She didn't get to see him very much, but he always acted as though they were long lost friends. Sammi Jo thought he was great. He was a major part of returning home. Things just wouldn't be the same without Karl at the door.

Karl wore a bright red jacket with big, shiny brass buttons that looked like little round mirrors all the way down the front. He wore a black top hat, black pants, and shiny black boots that were polished to such perfection that you could see your reflection. The best part of his "uniform" though, was his smile. It was always there. Whether he was sad or angry or happy or worried, his smile was always the same. He always said that he left his worries at the door when he got to work, and put on his best "uniform" smile for all his favorite people. Sammi Jo had never seen him without his uniform, and often wondered if she would actually recognize him if he were wearing something different.

The lobby was very elegant with marble floors, crystal chandeliers, and big comfy leather chairs and couches. There were tables with fresh flowers and a big brass coffee urn on a buffet against the wall. Karl's wife always made sure there were fresh cookies to go with the coffee. It was a very homey, comfy feeling lobby that was a quiet sanctuary after coming in from the hustle and bustle of the streets of New York. Karl made everyone feel welcome, and sometimes the residents of the apartment building would just sit in the lobby, drink coffee, read the newspaper, and visit with Karl.

The elevator doors were shiny brass mirrors. You could actually see yourself walking toward them. One of Karl's jobs was to keep those doors shiny and free of fingerprints. He did a fabulous job and never even got mad when children would put their grimy fingers all over his freshly polished doors. He would just laugh and start polishing them again. The inside of the elevator was just as shiny, with soft lights and quiet music playing in the background.

Sammi and her parents got into the elevator and Sammi pushed the button to the twentieth floor. Her father punched several buttons on the keypad.

"Do you remember when you couldn't reach that button?" asked Mr. Meriwether. "I would have to lift you up so that you could push the button, or you would cry."

"Yes, I remember," laughed Sammi Jo.

The elevator made it all the way to the twentieth floor without stopping once. Sometimes it would stop at other floors to let other people on or off, but today, they were the only ones riding. The doors opened silently to their cozy apartment.

Sammi Jo's apartment was considered the penthouse, because it was the only apartment on that floor and it was the top floor. That is why the door opened directly into their apartment and why her dad had to push special numbers on the keypad in the elevator. Only they, or someone with their code, could send the elevator to the twentieth floor.

Sammi Jo loved their apartment. It was filled with books and cozy leather couches and had a beautiful view of the city of New York. One whole wall of the living room was glass, and she felt like a bird as she stood up so high looking down at the city. They were so high up that the people far below looked like little ants scurrying busily around on their errands and the cars looked like little toys. When she went out on the balcony, she could just barely hear the sounds from below, cars honking and trains going by on the tracks in the distance. But when the wind was blowing, it seemed like you were all alone, up in the clouds, floating in the sky. It was magical and she loved it.

Sammi Jo raced to her bedroom next.

"Ohhhhh, it's just as beautiful as I remember!" she shouted as she twirled around on her thick pink carpet.

Sammi's bedroom was decorated exactly as she had asked. It looked like a princess's room in a castle: the walls were painted to look like castle walls; she had a big canopy bed that was so high she had to have little stairs to get up on it; the floors were covered with thick pink rugs and all the lights were fastened to the walls like glowing candles. She had stuffed animals everywhere, some were even bigger than she was. She loved her room and was always happy to be able to spend time here. She would play princess, listen to music, read books, and sometimes just sit at her window seat looking out at the view of New York below.

She would get to spend one week here before they left for the cottage. She and her parents always saw the sights of New York before they began their summer adventures at the shore. The time always passed too quickly as they tried to pack everything into the one week. They would go to the zoo, Central Park, the theater, shopping, and anything else they could think of. Even though they had done it all before, it always seemed new and exciting and there was always something to see that they had never seen before. Last year, they took a horse and carriage ride through Central Park and got to see the stables where the horses stay when they are not working. She wondered what they would get to see this year.

The week passed much too quickly, and soon, it was their final night in New York. They were all packed. All they had to do was put the suitcases in the car and start driving. Sammi Jo sat at her desk writing a letter to Kara.

Dear Kara,

We are finally packed and ready to take off for the New Hampshire shores. We are leaving really early in the morning so we can get to the cottage and get unpacked. Mom and dad hired someone to clean and stock the refrigerator and pantry so we won't have to do that when we get there. The cottage gets awfully dusty sitting empty for nine months every year! We are going to have a bonfire the first night, like we always do, so I hope the people they hired remembered to buy marshmallows and chocolate so we can have s'mores! I'm sure you remember that we always do that to celebrate our first night back at the shore. I am really looking forward to walking barefoot in the sand and falling asleep to the sound of waves crashing into the shore, but I wish you were going to be there to share it with me. I hope I will find someone to play with…Well, have a great vacation!

Love,
Sammi Jo

Baby Elephant

Saturday morning arrived and Sammi Jo and her parents rushed around getting breakfast, putting more things in their bags, and taking a last quick peak at the city before they piled everything in the elevator and headed to the lobby. Karl was already there, waiting for them, with steaming cups of coffee for her parents and a jug of chocolate milk for her. He had his "uniform" smile in place on his face as he helped them pile their suitcases in the car and warmly wished them a safe journey.

They finally got themselves settled into their seats and prepared to leave. Sammi Jo always brought lots of books and paper and pencils with her in the car because it was a long drive to their cottage and she needed lots to do so she wouldn't get too bored.

At last, they were ready to leave. Karl, once again, told them to have a fun and safe trip, and then waved good-bye to them as they pulled away from the curb and out into the New York traffic.

"Boy, I sure am glad I don't have to do this much," said Mr. Meriwether as a taxi honked his horn loudly at him. "I feel bad for the people who have to do this every day!"

"We'll be out of this soon," said Mrs. Meriwether, "and then it will be smooth sailing the rest of the way to the shore!"

Sammi Jo settled down with her new book and her pillow and prepared for the long drive. She knew they would stop along the way to stretch their legs and eat, and there was always some side trip that her mom would want to go on, but for now, she would just read for a while.

They had driven for about an hour when Sammi Jo sat up to look out the window. Her parents were listening to the radio and talking quietly when Sammi Jo exclaimed, "Oh my goodness, look at that!" Both her parents turned to look at what she was pointing at and saw, much to their amazement, a huge red and white striped tent just up ahead, off to the side of the road.

"Can we stop? Please, can we stop?" cried Sammi Jo.

"Well, sure I guess so", said her dad. "We've been making pretty good time. Let's stop and see what is going on!"

They pulled over in front of the tent and saw that there were several trailers, trucks, and smaller tents, all parked around and behind the big tent. There were people strolling around in all sorts of crazy outfits, and even a guy that was about ten feet tall!

"It's a circus!" screamed Sammi Jo.

She and her parents got out of the car and were greeted by a very silly looking clown with a monkey on his shoulder. "What can I help you with?" he asked.

"We were just wondering why there was a circus tent pitched out here so far away from town," asked her dad.

"Well, one of our elephants is getting ready to have a baby, so we had to stop for a while. We decided to set up the tent so that everyone else can practice their acts rather than just sit around waiting. Would you like me to show you around?"

"Yes, yes!" shouted Sammi Jo. "I want to look around!"

The clown smiled down at Sammi Jo and glanced toward her parents. Her dad just smiled and nodded his head and the clown took Sammi Jo's hand and headed toward the Big Top!

"My name is Clancy," said the clown. "What is your name?"

Sammi Jo told him her name and then stopped with her mouth open as they entered the Big Top. There were people and animals everywhere. There were trapeze artists flying through the air, dogs hopping through hoops, lions roaring from cages, horses with plumes on their heads with girls standing on their backs running in the large center ring. It was chaos and beautiful and loud and Sammi Jo just stood there, stock still, trying to take it all in.

"What's the matter, Sammi?" laughed her dad, "cat got your tongue?"

"No, I think it's a lion!" Sammi Jo said breathlessly.

Clancy took the Meriwether's from one place to another, introducing them to all the circus people and letting Sammi Jo pet whatever animals she could. She couldn't pet the lions, but she did get to stand really close to the cage and watch as the lion trainer made the lions turn circles and jump through hoops. Finally, Clancy took them to get some cotton candy and hot dogs.

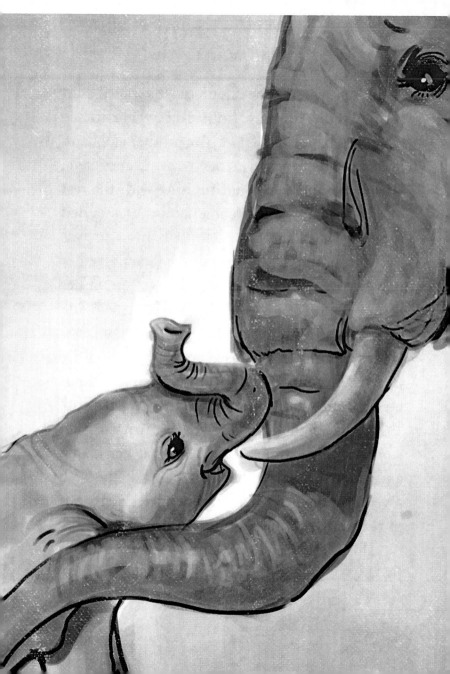

Suddenly, someone shouted, "It's a girl!" and people came running from everywhere to see what had happened. Clara, the mother elephant, had just given birth to her baby. Clancy said, "Let's go!" and they went running with the rest of the crowd to the elephant tent. Clancy led them through the crowd until Sammi Jo was right up front, just in time to see Clara give her new baby a nudge, and watch her get up on her little wobbly legs. It was incredible to see! The baby was so tiny, but so big compared to other babies Sammi Jo was used to seeing. The little baby walked straight over to her mama and put up her little truck to pat her mama on the head. "Ahhhhh," sighed the crowd. The veterinarian smiled a huge smile at the baby and her mama and then turned to the crowd to ask them to give her some privacy. Everyone filed quietly out of the tent with huge smiles on their faces.

"This is the BEST day EVER," sighed Sammi Jo. "I wish we could stay forever!"

"It has definitely been fun," said her mom, "but we do need to get back on the road or we won't make it to the cottage in time to have a bonfire!"

Everyone thanked Clancy for showing them all such a great time, and waved good-bye to all the rest of their new friends as they climbed back into the car to continue their journey. Sammi Jo was exhausted from all the excitement and fell asleep with a big smile on her face.

What's That Noise?

When Sammi Jo woke up, they were pulling into the driveway of their cottage. The waves were crashing onto the shore, the seagulls were flying overhead, and the smell of salt was in the air. It was very exciting to be back and they all piled out of the car, pulled off their shoes and wiggled their toes in the sand.

"Nothing feels quite as good as warm sand between your toes," sighed Sammi Jo's mom.

"Unless it's a warm fire and s'mores," said Sammi Jo. "Can we do it right now?"

"Not until after we get all of this stuff in the house and unpacked," said her dad. "Now shake a leg, so we can get finished before dark!"

It didn't take long to get everything unpacked and put away with everyone helping, and before she knew it, Sammi Jo was walking along the shore with her dad looking for driftwood to build a fire with.

"Make sure the wood is dry or it won't burn," said her dad as Sammi grabbed a large stick out of the water.

"I know," said Sammi Jo, "I just thought it was weird that this stick seemed to just fly here from somewhere. There was a splash and then this stick was here and it wasn't before." Sammi gazed out at the ocean as if she expected to see a large dog appear from the water wanting to fetch the stick, but nothing was there.

"That is strange," said her dad, "maybe it was stuck on something and just happened to pop up right then."

"Hmmmm, maybe," said Sammi Jo thoughtfully, as she continued to stare out at the ocean wonderingly while picking up more dry sticks for the fire.

By the time they got back to the house, her mom had gathered up hot dogs and marshmallows to roast over the fire, and graham crackers and chocolate to make the s'mores. Sammi Jo ran over to tell her mom about the mysterious stick, but since her mom didn't have any answers either, Sammi Jo soon forgot about it and they got busy building the fire. The sky was getting dark as the fire began to roar and Sammi Jo's mom handed hot dog sticks to everyone. They sat quietly for a while listening to the water and the sound and smell of their hot dogs sizzle over the fire. It was cozy and so familiar that Sammi Jo forgot all about how lonely she was for her friend and just appreciated the fact that she had such a fun and loving family.

Her dad began to groan, "Oh, I've eaten too many hot dogs, I think we should skip the s'mores for tonight."

"Oh, Daddy, your kid—" began Sammi Jo.

Right at that moment, there was a huge splash coming from the water.

"What was that?" exclaimed Sammi Jo and her mom at the same time.

"It was probably just a fish," said her dad staring out toward the dark water.

"No, it wasn't. That was way too loud!" shouted Sammi Jo.

They stood very still, listening, but heard nothing else. After a few moments, they decided to go ahead and start making their s'mores. They were all a little bit nervous and kept glancing toward the ocean wondering if they would see or hear something else.

"Let's sing a song," said her dad. "Does anyone remember our campfire songs from last summer?"

"I could teach you a new—" started Sammi Jo.

Splash!

"There it is again!" exclaimed Sammi Jo. "What is it, daddy?"

"Run up to the house and get my big floodlight, Sammi Jo, and we will see if we can see anything out there."

Sammi Jo went running to the house and appeared back, breathlessly, a few moments later with the floodlight. All three of them stood there with the flashlight for a very long time, but never saw or heard anything else. They finally decided to make their s'mores and go to bed. Mr. Meriwether said he would investigate in the morning when it was light to see if he could figure anything out.

They had their s'mores, sang some campfire songs, and gathered up all their things to take back to the house. There were no more noises.

Sammi Jo went to bed thinking that this was the *best day ever* and about what the noise could possibly have been. *Could it have been a whale? A dolphin? A sea monster? A wrecked ship?* she thought. She knew she would dream about it all night and couldn't wait to go out looking for evidence with her dad in the morning.

But first, she just had to get up and write to Kara.

Dear Kara,

We just got to the cottage today and I already have so many things to tell you. I just really wish you were here! On the way here, we got to get a tour of a circus that was set up on the side of the road. They were waiting for a baby elephant to be born, so they set up their tents for everyone to practice while they were waiting on the new baby. It was born while we there! It was so cute and tiny! You would have loved it! We finally got back on the road and made it to the cottage in time to have our bonfire and s'mores. We roasted hot dogs, too! But, the best part is that we have a *mystery*! We kept hearing these strange splashes the whole time we were having our bonfire, but we couldn't ever see anything. Daddy is going to explore with me in the morning and then I will tell you all about what we find!

I hope you are having fun, too! Write me soon and tell me all about Europe!

Love,
Sammi Jo

A Mysterious Find

Sammi Jo woke up in the morning feeling excited and ready to go on an adventure. She got dressed and ran to the kitchen. Her mom was cooking breakfast and her dad was staring out the window toward the sea.

"When can we go, Daddy?" asked Sammi Jo.

"Just as soon as we've had breakfast, honey," replied her dad. "But, I can't spend all day doing this, I have a deadline on my new novel and I will need to get to work soon."

"Okay, Daddy! Let's just hurry and eat, okay?

Sammi Jo's had made them pancakes and bacon and fruit for breakfast. They ate as quickly as they could and then headed down to the beach. They walked and walked and searched and searched, but found nothing out of the ordinary. They found shells and seaweed and hermit crabs and sand diggers, but nothing that shouldn't be there. They stared at the water for so long they began to see spots in front of their eyes, but still nothing. There were no more splashes; there was nothing mysterious or strange, only birds, crabs, water, sand, and seashells.

"Maybe it only comes out at night," said Sammi Jo.

"Maybe *what* only comes out at night?" asked her dad.

"Whatever made the noise, Daddy."

"We don't know that anything made the noise, honey. There was a noise, but it was probably just a fish or a whale or a dolphin trying to enjoy our fire with us. We are probably making way more out of this than we should. I need to get back to the house now and get to work, but you can keep exploring by yourself if you want," said her dad.

When they reached the house, Meriwether was already busy at work on her latest book, but she had packed a lunch for Sammi Jo and a note telling her to have fun, don't go past the point where she couldn't be seen from the house, and check back in soon. Mrs. Meriwether's office was in a small room with lots of windows facing the ocean. That way she could enjoy the sea, keep an eye out on Sammi Jo, and still get her work done.

Mr. Meriwether went to work in his office on the third floor of the house. It was in a room that was kind of like a tower and you had to go up a circular staircase to get to it. It was round and was surrounded by windows. He always said he felt like he was a bird sitting in his perch when he was working up there.

Sammi Jo put on a swimsuit, put her lunch in her backpack along with some water, her sunscreen and a shovel for digging in the sand, and set out to explore the beach. She looked forward to doing this every summer, because she always found interesting "treasures" that had washed up on shore. This year would be especially exciting since she was sure that she had a mystery to solve. Sammi Jo just *knew* that the splashes they had heard the night before were not ordinary splashes, and she was determined to find out what they were all about.

Sammi Jo scampered down the beach, enjoying the sunshine on her head and the warm sand on her feet. She could just feel the new freckles popping out on her nose. She walked near the water's edge so that the little waves could lap at her toes as the waves rolled in and laughed as they sometimes splashed up around her knees. Sammi Jo loved the shore and wasn't even lonely yet since she had so much to think about and explore. It would have been fun to have Kara with her, but she would make the best of it and look forward to writing Kara and telling her all about her treasures, especially if she really did discover the "mystery of the splash."

For a while, Sammi Jo just picked up pretty shells and pieces of broken glass and wood.

She found a few small sand diggers that would quickly bury themselves in the sand when she got near, and she even got chased by a couple of large sand crabs that were intent on biting her bare toes. Sammi Jo just laughed and ran away. She knew that they couldn't catch her unless she just stood still and let them.

After a while, she began to get tired and thirsty and hungry, so she found a shady spot with a nice view of the ocean. She noticed that there was a huge rock sticking up out of the ocean not too far from shore and decided to ask her parents if they would come with her so she could swim out to the rock with them. It would be a great place for a picnic lunch and she knew she couldn't go out there by herself. So, she just kept staring at it and wondering what it would feel like to be sitting on top of it, surrounded by water.

It would be just like having my own little island, she thought to herself, and then gasped as she saw *something* peek around the rock and then disappear just as quickly. *What was that?* she thought to herself, and then wondered if the sun was simply playing tricks with her eyes. She gazed intently at the little rock island while she munched slowly on her apple. Hopefully, whatever it was would appear again. But as hard as she stared, she saw nothing but the water and the rock...did she really see something or was it simply her overactive imagination?

Sammi Jo got tired of staring at the rock, so quickly finished up her lunch, gathered up all her trash, and began her treasure seeking again. She had not gone far when something flashed at the water's edge and she rushed over to see what it could be. Lying just at the water's edge was a large, flat, shiny object. It had a multitude of colors, all swirled together like a big pot of water colors that had all melted together, and it shined and twinkled in the bright sunlight. Sammi Jo picked it up and turned it over slowly in her hands. The "treasure" was about as big as her hand and kind of smooth and leathery feeling.

It wasn't quite hard, but not real soft either, and it kind of molded to her hand as she held it. It almost felt alive, but she could tell it wasn't an animal. Sammi Jo had never seen anything like this in her life and had no idea what it could possibly be. *I wonder if daddy will know what it is?* she thought to herself as she slowly turned it over and over in her hands.

As she was pondering her new find, she saw something move out of the corner of her eye, and quickly glanced up toward the rock island again, only to find nothing—again. *I know there is something out there, but how am I going to catch what it is?* she wondered. "Hello? Is someone there?" she called out. But nothing appeared and she stared so long that her eyes began to water, and she had to close her eyes for a minute. When she re-opened them, she saw a huge pair of eyes peering around the side of the rock, their eyes locked for a moment and then the big eyes blinked and disappeared behind the rock. "Hey, come back!" Sammi Jo hollered. "I won't hurt you, please come back!" She pleaded and pleaded for the eyes to reappear, but whomever or whatever those eyes had belonged to, had gone. She wondered if her mysterious shell thing had something to do with the disappearing eyes behind the rock.

It was getting late and her stomach was beginning to growl, so she added her newest treasure to her backpack, and started to head home after glancing back toward the rock one more time. Maybe her mom or dad would be able to shed some light on what she had found, and she couldn't wait to tell them about what she saw, or thought she saw behind the rock island. *Maybe I'll be able to discover what is hiding behind the rock tomorrow,* she hoped as she solemnly crossed her fingers and continued her walk back home.

"Mom, Dad!" she called as walked into the house. "Wait 'til you see what I found!"

"You sure seem excited," her mom replied as she poked her head around the kitchen door, where she was getting dinner ready. "What happened today to get you so fired up?"

"I'll tell you both as soon as dad gets here, but it was the ***best day ever!***" said Sammi Jo as she smiled mysteriously at her mom. "I can't wait to go back tomorrow!"

Dear Kara,

Oh my goodness! The mystery is really growing! Today I was exploring the beach and I found this really strange shell. It's not really a shell, but it kind of looks like a shell. It has tons of different colors that all run together and it is kind of soft. And it kind of feels alive! But, the strangest thing was that I found it near this little rock island that is off the shore and while I was looking at the island, I could've sworn that I saw a pair of eyes looking back at me! I sure wish you were here to explore with me, but I will let you know as soon as I learn something new. I just know that it is going to be the coolest thing ever!

Love,
Sammi Jo

A New Friend

Sammi Jo woke up bright and early. She lay there for a few minutes thinking about the conversation she had had with her parents the night before. Both her parents had agreed that there was a mystery at hand, but neither of them had any clue of what it might be. They encouraged her to put her detective abilities to use and figure out what was out there. Sammi also saw them smile at each other in a mysterious fashion. She knew that they didn't believe her, but were simply indulging her fantasies and imagination. *That's okay*, she thought to herself, *I will discover*

*what is going on and they will be astounded, I just
know it!*

She jumped out of bed and got dressed and
ready to start today's new adventure. Today, she
would discover the mystery of the strange "flying
stick," the "shell," the "splash," and the "big eyes"
peering around the side of the rock island. She
just knew it.

Sammi Jo ran down the stairs to greet her
parents and eat breakfast before starting out to
complete her quest for the day.

"Good morning, Mom, Dad! What's
for breakfast?"

"You sure are bright-eyed today," exclaimed
her dad. "Got big plans for the day?"

"I sure do! I am going to figure out the mystery
today and will have proof for you by the time I
get home!" said Sammi Jo excitedly.

"Well, I will be waiting to see what you
discover! I'm sure that you will be able to figure
this out. I just hope that it is exciting as you
seem to think it will be," said her mom.

"Oh, it will be," her dad muttered. "With her imagination, it's bound to be quite a story!"

"You'll see," said Sammi Jo, "it will be something awesome. You just wait and see…"

Sammi Jo ate her breakfast of cereal and strawberries, packed up her backpack for the day and assured her parents that she would not go beyond the point. She headed out the door, eager to start today's explorations.

"I sure hope that she discovers something worthwhile," said Meriwether, "I would hate for her to be too disappointed if there is nothing more than a big fish out there."

"Whatever it is, she will make it exciting," replied Mr. Meriwether. "You know how she can turn anything into a wonderful story. I'm sure she will be a writer when she grows up!"

They both laughed, remembering some of Sammi Jo's previous adventures and stories, and then went to their offices to begin their work for the day.

Sammi Jo hurried toward her rock island in anticipation of what she might find today. On the way, she scouted for any new clues that she might find. She found all the normal stuff that she would normally find, so continued on her way. She just knew that she would find or discover something new and exciting today!

She chose to set up her "observation point" at the same place where she had eaten lunch yesterday. It was comfy under the tree and it blocked some of the bright sun, while still allowing her to keep a close eye on the little rock island. She knew that she had seen some eyes peering around the rock yesterday and she was determined to see the same thing today. But today, she would discover what was behind those eyes.

She spread out her blanket and made a cozy area to "set up camp" and then pulled the odd shell from her backpack. As soon as she touched it, she had the same sensation that she had had before. It did not feel like a shell, it felt…alive.

She knew this was strange, but that is what it felt like. *Whatever could it be?* she thought to herself. *It's not a shell, it's not an animal…but it almost feels like it's breathing…*

Splash!

Sammi Jo jumped up from her blanket and looked toward the island. Again…nothing. She **knew** something was there, and it was obviously curious about her as well. How could she coax it from behind the rock? She searched through her backpack to see what might work. *I wonder if it would like an apple?* She took an apple out and walked down to the edge of the waterline, tenderly setting it right at the edge of the water. After seeing nothing, she turned and walked back to her blanket and lowered herself slowly to the ground. She glanced lazily at the place where she had left the apple…*it was gone*!

"Oh my goodness, I only had my back turned for a minute!" she exclaimed out loud. "Maybe the water pulled it away…but no, I made sure it was where the water couldn't reach it," Sammi

Jo muttered to herself. "What can I try next? I don't have any more apples. Let's see…" She began to rummage through her backpack to see what she might find. She stored all sorts of treasures in there because you just never know when something might come in handy. "Aha!" she shouted. "A ball! Maybe it would like to play ball," she laughed, but took the ball out anyway and slowly walked to the water's edge again, tossing the ball up and down in her hand as she went. She tried to look really bored, so that whatever was watching her wouldn't get spooked again. She just stood there, tossing the ball up and down, up and down, while she stared intently at the rock island, and sure enough the eyes appeared, but only for a second. "Yippee!" shouted Sammi Jo. "There is something out there and it wants to know me too, I just *know* it!"

"Wanna play ball?" shouted Sammi. "I have one right here, just come out and I'll toss it to you!" But nothing happened. She waited...and waited...and waited...and waited, but nothing. "Please, come out!" she shouted. "I promise I won't hurt you." And then, something small and shiny flew out of the water and landed at her feet. Sammi pounced on it eagerly. It was another one of the strange shells. Whomever or whatever was out there *definitely* had something to do with her finding the first shell, and now it just threw her another one. *This will prove it to my parents*, she thought to herself. But how in the world was she going to convince it to come out? *Maybe...if I throw something of mine back... maybe it will be like a trade or something*, Sammi Jo thought as she bounced her ball up and down. She stared intently at the rock island, pulled her arm back, and threw her little red ball as hard and as far as she possibly could. It landed just a little beyond the island (the wind was blowing toward the island, so it carried the ball further than what it should've gone), and bobbed up and down on the little waves…bobbing…bobbing…bobbing…just like the apples you bob for in the fall festivals they have at school…and then it was gone! Just like that! She had hardly even blinked, but the ball was no longer bobbing on the waves…it was gone.

"Where are you?" hollered Sammi, "please show yourself…please!" And as she gazed longingly at the rock, something wondrous began to happen. Slowly, the big eyes began to peep around the side of the rock and then even more slowly, the large bluish green head that went with those eyes and then the cheeks…and then the long nose and finally a *huge* mouth, holding the red ball. It stared at her for a long moment and then tossed its head and the red ball came sailing right back at Sammi Jo. Sammi lunged to catch the ball and then turned quickly to look back toward the rock and the strange creature hiding behind it. The creature stared for another long moment and then with a loud *splash*, disappeared.

Sammi Jo stood rooted to the spot for so long that her feet began to get covered up with water as the tide began to come back in. She realized that it was late and she had better be heading back home, but she would return again tomorrow, and tomorrow she just knew that she would get to see more of her new "very shy" friend.

Sammi grabbed her backpack and raced towards home.

She burst into the kitchen tossing her backpack on the floor and scattering sand everywhere.

"Mom, Dad! You are never going to believe what happened today! This was *definitely* the *best day ever!*"

Sammi told her parents the whole story, while they oohed and aahed in amazement at Sammi Jo's newest story. They were so proud of her detective abilities and encouraged her to find out more. They even got out some books about the sea animals in their area to see if there was anything like it in any of the books, but the closest they could come up with were prehistoric animals that had been dead for millions of years.

Sammi finally went to bed, so excited that she could hardly sleep. And when she did sleep, her dreams were full of big eyes, green faces, and red balls. Tomorrow would be an even better day. She just knew it.

Dear Kara,

You are never going to believe this! I was back on the beach today trying to figure out what the shell is and to see if I could see those eyes again and…well, not only did I see the eyes again, but I saw the head that goes with those eyes! It is some sort of sea creature and it is kind of a greenish blue, with a mouth that looks like a duck and really long eyelashes. I threw my ball into the water and the creature actually threw it back to me! The only kind of sea creatures that we could find in the books we have at home are extinct and have been gone for millions of years…so, what could it be?

Love,
Sammi Jo

Screech

Sammi Jo's eyes popped open and she jumped out of bed in a flash. Today would be the day that she would see the rest of her mysterious new "friend." She pulled on her clothes as fast as she could and went barreling down the stairs so fast that she missed the last two steps and went sprawling across the landing.

"I'm okay!" she shouted as she pulled herself up off the floor, laughing. "I'm just in a hurry to get down the beach."

"Well, if you keep that up you'll break a leg before you make it down there," boomed her dad. "Take care so you can pursue your dream of the day."

"I will, Dad. Where's Mom? What's for breakfast?"

"Mom is outside looking for some early morning clams and your cereal is on the table. I'll make you some sandwiches to take with you if you want," said her dad.

"Sure, thanks Dad!"

Sammi Jo poured out her cereal and downed her glass of orange juice so fast that she was done before her dad even finished making her peanut butter sandwiches.

"Are you finished yet?" asked Sammi Jo. "I'd really like to get started."

"Hold your horses, Sammi. I'll be done in a second."

Within minutes, Sammi Jo had her backpack ready to go, stuffed in her sandwiches and apples and some water, waved goodbye to her dad and took off down to the beach.

I so hope that the creature is there today, she wished to herself as she crossed her fingers tightly together. *I just know it will be back, I just know it!*

She approached her little beach area cautiously, peering anxiously at the rock island, but she didn't see anything yet.

That's okay, it is still early, she thought to herself. *I have all day to find him or her or it.*

Sammi Jo spread out her beach towel and sat down facing the rock island. She had brought a book to pass the time, so she took that out of her backpack too and set it on the towel beside her. She took out two apples and her red ball while casting anxious glances at the rock island. Several minutes passed while she placed everything around her and then she sighed out loud, "What am I going to do if it doesn't show up today? I'm all ready and I really need to find a friend to play with and talk to..." She slowly picked up her book and opened it to the last page she had read. *Perhaps*, she thought, *if I get busy reading I will forget about watching and waiting and the time will pass a lot faster.* As her mom always said, "A watched pot never boils," meaning, of course, that the more you wait and worry, the longer it seems to take for it—whatever it is—to happen.

Sammi Jo began reading her book and before too long was so wrapped up in her story that she forgot to keep an eye out on the island. She had just reached a very exciting part of her story, when…*splash!*

She threw down her book and jumped to her feet. And looking around the side of the rock were the big eyes. It was back! Sammi was so excited, she didn't know what to do, so she just stood and stared, with her mouth hanging open, hoping, just hoping that it would reveal more of itself if she stood very still.

Slowly, the creature moved forward, inch by inch, until Sammi Jo could see its whole head, and then a neck began to appear. It was *very* long and covered in the most beautiful greenish, bluish scales. The scales looked exactly like the strange "shell" that she had found on the beach that very first day. "It wasn't a shell," she breathed softly to herself, "it was a scale. No wonder it seemed to be alive."

As the creature began to reveal more and more of itself, Sammi Jo's excitement grew and grew as she gazed in wonder at something she was sure no one else had ever seen. The back of its neck had fins or something like fins sticking up from it that were also a greenish, bluish color, and as its entire body began to appear, she could see its tail, which also had the fins and the beautiful iridescent scales. Before too long, its entire body was revealed around the side of the rock. It gazed back at Sammi Jo and appeared to be just as interested in her and she was in it. After several long moments, it lifted its long beautiful tail and *splash* as it slapped the water. The *mysterious* splash…this was what she had been hearing ever since the first night at the bonfire. It certainly wasn't a dolphin or a whale.

Sammi Jo slowly lifted her hand and waved at the unusual creature and was astounded that it lifted a big flipper out of the water and seemed to wave back at her as it opened its mouth and emitted a high pitched squeal, *Screeeeeeeeeeccccchhhhh!* The sound was so loud, that Sammi Jo had to cover her ears.

"Oh my goodness!" she exclaimed, "What was that?"

Screeeeeeeecccchhhhh! It squealed again.

"Is that your name?" asked Sammi Jo.

It nodded its head up and down very fast!

"So, that's what I will call you then. Screech. Is that okay with you?" she asked.

Again, it nodded its head up and down.

"Do you understand me?" Sammi Jo asked wonderingly.

It nodded again and batted its big eyelashes at her.

"So, your name is Screech and you understand what I am saying. This is unbelievable!"

And then in a very high pitched, squeaky kind of voice, it said, "And what is your name?"

"Oh my goodness!" exclaimed Sammi Jo, "you can speak in English? My name is Sammi Jo, and how do you know how to speak my language?"

"I've been watching and listening to humans for years," it answered. "You pick up a few things if you remain quiet and just listen."

"Are you a boy or a girl?" asked Sammi Jo.

"I'm a boy!" he exclaimed. "If I was a girl, my scales would be pink and gray instead of blue and green. My mom has got beautiful pink scales!"

"Have you made friends with other humans?" asked Sammi Jo.

"No, you are the first," Screech answered.

"But, why me?"

"Because you were the only one to pay attention to the clues!" he answered. "I have been waiting for many years for a human child to be observant enough to look for what was out here. You are the first to figure out that the splashes and the shell were different and to attempt to figure it out."

"Wow!" exclaimed Sammi Jo. "The only reason I even paid attention is because I don't have any friends here, and because it seemed to be a mystery for me to solve. I love solving mysteries!"

"You have no idea what mysteries can be found in the ocean. Strange fish, sunken boats, treasures, lost cities, and so many other things!" said Screech.

"Oh, that sounds so wonderful," sighed Sammi Jo. "I sure wish I could see them all with you."

"And you can," said Screech mysteriously. "If you want to…"

At that exact moment, Sammi Jo could hear her dad calling for her from far away. She turned to look and *splash*, Screech was gone.

Sammi Jo grabbed her backpack, shoved all of her things inside quickly, and went running towards home.

"You will never guess what happened today!" she screamed at her dad, breathlessly as she ran up to the house. "Today was the *absolute BEST day EVER!*"

Dear Kara,

It finally happened! I met the creature! He even has a name! He was making this horrible high pitched screeching noise, so I decided to call him Screech. He can talk! He told me how he learned to speak English, about how to tell the difference between boys and girls and about the wondrous adventures and mysteries found in the ocean. He even hinted at how I could go with him, but then he got scared and disappeared. I hope he will tell me all about it tomorrow.

My parents think my imagination has run wild, but it is all true! I will tell you more later.

Love,
Sammi Jo

A Shell Phone on a Stormy Day

Again, Sammi Jo rushed to head out the door early. She grabbed her backpack right after finishing her breakfast and darted for the door.

"Whoa there, little girl," boomed her dad. "Why are you rushing off so fast?"

"I have to go and meet Screech!" exclaimed Sammi Jo. "Today, I hope, we are going on an adventure."

"You have been spending an awful lot of time at the beach and no time doing your chores." said her dad. "Before you head out today, you need to get your chores done. Take out the trash, make your bed, and help me with the breakfast dishes, and then you can head out to your adventure."

"But…"

"No buts, allowed. Do your chores and then you can go."

Sammi sadly dropped her backpack and set about her chores, she made her bed and straightened up her room, emptied all the trash cans in the house and took the bags out to the big trash cans in the garage, cleared the table and washed the dishes while her dad dried them and put them away. Finally, she was finished with everything.

"May I go now, Dad?"

"Yes, you may," announced her dad. "Don't have too much fun," he laughed. But before he could even get a response, Sammi Jo had grabbed her backpack and disappeared.

It was already almost ten in the morning and Sammi Jo was in such a hurry that she didn't even notice that the sun was obscured by clouds today and it was getting windy. She just rushed to the beach to eagerly await Screech while keeping her fingers crossed that he would actually show up today.

By the time she arrived, the sky was getting darker and the waves were getting bigger, but Sammi Jo didn't mind; she loved stormy days and watching the big waves come crashing to the shore. She just hoped that it wouldn't stop Screech from coming so close to shore.

Things seemed a bit different today and she didn't see Screech at all. There was a very large seashell at the water's edge that she hadn't seen before so she wandered over to pick it up, and under it was a beautiful pink scale. It had to be some sort of a message from Screech. And the pink scale had to belong to his mom.

She cautiously put the seashell up to her ear, expecting to hear the normal ocean sounds that one usually hears when they put a shell up to their ears, but instead she heard Screech's voice. He was using the shell to communicate with her!

"Hi, Sammi Jo! This is Screech. This shell is a way we can talk to each other when we need to. As long as you are near the water and have the shell, we can talk directly and if I am not near, it will save whatever you say so that I can hear it later. Right now, I am way out of range, so I have left you this message. There is a BIG storm coming, so I have had to go far out into deeper water with my parents. You should go home, too, if you are at the beach. I hope that we can see each other tomorrow. Keep this shell safe. I have a matching one, but if either of us loses our shell, we will have to find a new matching shell set to talk on. Stay safe and go home quickly!"

"Hi back, Screech. This is so awesome! I am sad that I can't see you today, but I will rush home and hope to see you tomorrow. I will keep my shell in my backpack, so I will never lose it. I hope you stay safe. See you tomorrow, hopefully!"

Sammi Jo placed the shell carefully in her backpack, took a quick look at the sky and raced home as fast as she could.

Her parents were waiting anxiously on the porch and her mom heaved a huge sigh of relief when Sammi Jo dashed up the porch stairs.

"I was so worried," exclaimed her mom. "Thank goodness you had the good sense to come home."

"Screech left me a message about the storm, so I rushed home as quickly as I could!" announced Sammi Jo.

"How did he leave you a message?" asked her dad.

Sammi Jo pulled out the seashell and told him to hold it to his ear.

"All I hear is the sea," said her dad. "What am I supposed to be hearing?"

"There is a message from Screech telling me about the storm and that I should go home," said Sammi Jo. "Can't you hear it?"

"No, just the sounds of the sea," replied her dad.

Just at that moment, there was a huge clap of thunder as lightning raced across the sky and the lights went off.

"I guess we are having a day in the dark," commented her mom. "How about hot dogs over the fire?"

"That would be great," replied Sammi Jo. "Do we still have chocolate and marshmallows? We could do s'mores again and tell stories."

"I believe that we do," said her mom. "Since our computers won't work without electricity that sounds like a pretty fun way to spend our day."

Sammi Jo's mom set about gathering up food and blankets to lay in front of the fireplace while her dad found the candles and lanterns. He kept glancing anxiously out the window, but their house was far enough back from the beach to avoid the huge waves that were billowing up onto the shore.

The winds were bending the sea grasses flat to the ground, and the sand was blowing so hard that they could not even attempt to go outside. It was cozy in the house, even though the gusts of wind would sometimes make the house shiver as though it had a cold. Sammi Jo and her parents settled down to spend the afternoon with each other in their safe haven.

Sammi Jo began to tell her parents the whole story about Screech. They glanced at each other with glances that showed that they did not believe a word that she said. They both began to tell her stories about their "imaginary friends" that they had as children. No matter how much Sammi Jo persisted, they still would not believe Screech was real. Sammi Jo finally gave up and just let them tell their stories. Obviously, her relationship with Screech would be one that she alone would enjoy.

When they got bored with telling stories, they pulled out some board games and passed the time playing games until suppertime when they cooked hot dogs over the fireplace. They followed the hot dogs with s'mores and finally popcorn before bed. It was a nice and cozy day, but Sammi Jo really hoped the weather would improve before tomorrow so that she could see what kind of adventures Screech had planned for them.

Absolutely, Positively the Best Day Ever!

The next morning dawned bright and beautiful. The sky was a clear blue and the only signs of the previous day's storm were the seaweed and shells that were scattered all over the beach.

Sammi Jo jumped out of bed and ran to the window. "Yay, I can go to the beach today!" she exclaimed to herself. She rushed to pull on her swimsuit, shorts, and a t-shirt, and raced down the stairs for breakfast.

"Mornin' punkin," bellowed her dad. "Beautiful day for a picnic. Are you planning on meeting your friend today?"

"You bet," exclaimed Sammi Jo. "We are going on an exciting adventure."

"Just make sure you don't go too far and watch for any signs of bad weather. We don't want you to get stuck somewhere if the weather turns bad like it did yesterday."

"I'll be careful, Daddy. Screech is really aware of the weather; he's the one who told me to come home yesterday. I'm going to take some extra apples along, okay?" asked Sammi Jo.

"Whatever you want, honey. Have a wonderful day. Don't be late for dinner," said her dad. "And be careful," he exclaimed as he gave her his very stern look.

"Okay, Dad," laughed Sammi Jo. "See you tonight!"

Sammi Jo grabbed her backpack and headed out the door. She was so excited, she tripped and fell flat on the porch. She jumped up, laughing at herself, and ran carefully down the porch steps.

Running toward the beach, her mind was so full of what could be in store for the day, that it took her several moments to notice the strange noises coming from her backpack.

Bubble...bubble...bubble. It sounded like the washing machine or a bubble blower or ... something...Sammi stopped and opened her backpack and noticed the "shell phone" Screech had left her yesterday was vibrating. She picked it up very carefully and put it to her ear.

"Hello?" she said very cautiously.

"Where are you?" asked Screech in his strange, high-pitched voice. "I've been waiting, forever!"

"Almost there," laughed Sammi Jo, thinking how strange it was to be talking to a creature from the sea on a shell that is usually the home to another sea creature.

She bounded onto her little beach to see Screech peering out from behind the rock island. His eyes were huge and he was practically bouncing with impatience.

Sammi Jo waved at him and he slid quickly out from his hiding place and came as close to the shore as he could.

"Are you ready for this?" he asked.

"Absolutely! I was so sad that we couldn't go yesterday, but am sure excited to go today! How are we going to do this? I can't breathe underwater, you know."

"I know, I know," said Screech. "Hold on for a minute. Can you swim?"

"Of course I can swim," said Sammi Jo indignantly. "Do you think my parents would let me come to the beach all by myself if I couldn't? They had me in swimming lessons ever since I was a little baby. I could swim before I could walk. They knew that we would spend a lot of time near water and wanted me to be a strong swimmer so that they could be sure that I could save myself if I needed to."

"Great!" said Screech. "Do you still have one of the scales that you found?"

"Yes," said Sammi Jo.

"Okay. You can use either mine or the pink one of my mom's. My mom's might be a little big, so try mine first. Put it over your mouth and nose and take a deep breath."

Sammi Jo pulled the original scale she had found out of her backpack and cautiously put it up to her face. She took a deep breath and it quickly transformed into a perfectly fitting mask.

"Wow!" she shouted. "This is so cool! I can even talk."

"When we get into the water, all you need to do is breathe normally. The scale will work like an oxygen mask for you," explained Screech. "You will sit on my back and hold on to my fins and I will show you my home!"

"What if we run into sharks or something like that?" asked Sammi Jo cautiously.

"I am bigger than anything out here," said Screech. "There is absolutely nothing that will bother you as long as you are with me. Just hold on tight and enjoy the ride."

"Okay," said Sammi Jo. "Here I come!"

She waded into the water and then swam the rest of the distance to where Screech was waiting for her and climbed onto his back.

His scales were soft and leathery and she quickly found a comfortable spot that was not too wide for her legs to go around him, and also close enough to his head that she could still talk with him. She grabbed hold of one of his fins and declared herself ready to go.

"My mom would really like you to come visit our home for this first adventure. Is that okay?" asked Screech.

"Of course," said Sammi Jo. "Just wait until I tell Kara that I got to meet a sea serpent's mom in her underwater home. She'll never believe it!"

"Here we go," said Screech. "If you get nervous or scared, just tap on my side really hard, since it will be harder to hear you when I am swimming. I will come up top right away."

"OKAY! I'm ready!" hollered Sammi Jo, excitedly.

Screech swam out into deeper water and quickly submerged. Sammi Jo's world quickly transformed into a bluish green haze and she stared in wonder at all of the things she had never seen before.

There were tall plants growing from the bottom of the sea and beautiful corals of all different colors and shapes. There were schools of small fish swarming all around them in dozens of different colors and shapes. They all seemed to be very curious and started following her and Screech as they swam deeper and further into the sea.

The fish began to get larger as they got deeper, and she did get a little nervous when an enormous grouper swam up beside them to get a closer look at Sammi Jo.

She knew that she was safe with Screech and after a little bit, she began to relax. She waved at the fish and giggled when the smaller ones would swim in front of her face as if they were trying to figure out what that strange creature was on Screech's back.

He took her through tunnels made out of natural sea formations and slowed down when they came to a particular area full of tall grass and ferns.

"Look closely," he said softly, "and see what you can find."

Sammi Jo peered closely at the leaves and gasped as she saw dozens and dozens of small seahorses clinging to the leaves and waving slowly back and forth with the current. She had seen seahorses in aquariums before, but this was amazing. They looked so much like real horses, except they had no legs, and their tails curled around the leaves as though they were tied to hitching post.

"These are the kind that humans usually see," explained Screech, "but one of these days, I will show you the seahorses that no one but you will ever lay eyes on."

He swam on, occasionally slowing down to show her something exceptionally beautiful, and they eventually arrived at a huge underwater cave. He slowly swam to the surface while Sammi Jo gazed in wonder at the walls that were covered with sparkling gems and small shiny sea creatures. She had never seen anything so beautiful in her life.

"Here we are!" Screech exclaimed as they surfaced.

Sammi Jo's head came out of the water and her mouth dropped open as she found herself in one of the most gigantic caverns she had ever seen or thought of. The water was sparkling blue and there were pinpoints of lights sparkling from all over. It looked like there were stars pinned all over the ceiling, causing the entire cavern to be lit up like a beautiful clear night sky. There was also a little shore area which Screech swam up to for Sammi Jo to get off his back.

Sammi dismounted and stood on the little beach; she took her mask off and was able to breathe normally, while she continued to stare in wonder.

"This is amazing, Screech! Where are we? Is this your home? Where are your parents? Do you sleep here? Is this where you come after you leave me? Do you have a bed? What do you eat?"

"Slow down," laughed Screech. "All of your questions will get answered. But for now, have a seat and get prepared…I don't want you to be afraid. My parents are MUCH larger than I am, but they are excited to meet you and would never hurt you. They are not able to speak your language, except for a couple of words that I have taught them, so don't feel bad if they don't say much."

Sammi Jo sat and pulled her knees up to her chest, nervously. She didn't really know what to expect, but waited patiently for whatever was about to happen. She also took out the extra apples she had packed that morning and placed them on the sand beside her. She had thought that since Screech seemed to like the apples so much, it might be a nice gift for his parents.

Screech disappeared under the water and for a short period of time, Sammi Jo was alone in the beautiful cave. She wasn't afraid, she knew Screech would be back and she couldn't wait to see what, or who, would be with him.

After several long moments, she began to see the water move. The ripples were incredibly long and she waited anxiously to see what would come up. Screech's head popped out of the water first, and he looked at her and smiled mysteriously as slowly some *much* bigger eyes began to appear out of the water. These were followed by a *much, much* bigger face and mouth. The scales were mostly pink, but mixed with all of the pastel colors one could ever imagine. As the rest of her face and neck began to appear, Sammi Jo realized that Screech must be very young as his mom was at least twice the size of him. When her entire neck appeared, she had to bend her neck in half to look Sammi Jo directly in the face.

Her *huge* eyes gazed directly into Sammi Jo's small human eyes and she gently nudged her face as if to say hello.

Sammi Jo slowly leaned over to pick up an apple to hand to her in greeting. Screech's mom took it gently from Sammi Jo's outstretched hand and swallowed it whole. She bobbed her head in thanks and then moved aside.

Another, even larger head was emerging from the water. This one looked much more like Screech, with the same blue and green scales. This had to be Screech's dad. He also moved very slowly and cautiously up to examine Sammi Jo. He bent his long neck and peered at her face and then gently nudged her shoulder and sniffed at her red pigtails, blowing gently out his nostrils at her.

Sammi Jo handed him another one of her apples, and he took it from her gently, tossed it up in the air, opened his mouth, and neatly caught and swallowed it. He bobbed his head in thanks and moved over to wait beside his wife.

"Oh my goodness," breathed Sammi Jo to Screech. "They are incredible! Have they ever seen a human before?"

"Only from a distance," explained Screech. "They are a lot more cautious than I am. Humans have been trying to find us for years, but we are pretty good at staying hidden and most humans could never come this deep."

Screech's mom disappeared for a moment and then reappeared with some large leafy plants and shells, which she laid at Sammi Jo's feet.

"What is this?" asked Sammi Jo.

"This is lunch," answered Screech. "My mom wanted to make sure that you felt welcome and wanted you to see what we eat. There are many different types of seaweed and shellfish that we like to eat, but these are my mom's favorites."

Sammi Jo took a cautious bite of the seaweed, and although it was certainly not what she was used to, it wasn't bad. It tasted very salty and fishy, but also crunchy like a salad her mom would make.

"How do I eat the shellfish?" she asked.

"Pick one up and smash it on the rocks, and then you can pick out the meat with your fingers," explained Screech.

Sammi Jo did as she was told and devoured the small shellfish whole. She had had oysters and clams and mussels before, but this was totally different. Obviously, the shellfish that her parents buy at seafood markets did not come from waters this deep.

"Thank you very much," she said to Screech's mom. "Lunch was delicious!"

Screech's mom, bobbed her head, and seemed to smile back at Sammi Jo.

Screech's dad also wanted to give Sammi Jo a gift, so he reached up toward the walls with his long neck and pulled one of the "stars" from the cavern wall. He bent down slowly to place it in Sammi Jo's hand.

Sammi Jo gasped as she stared at it. It looked like a perfectly formed diamond of some sort, but it gave off a soft glow like a small night-light. It was beautiful and she would treasure it forever.

"Oh, thank you!" she breathed softly. "I love it!"

He also bobbed his head and smiled at Sammi Jo.

It was obvious that both of his parents were just as excited to see her as she was to see them.

Screech had her get back on his back and gave her the underwater tour of his home. There were many smaller caverns and caves hidden in the cave walls and they explored all of them, while his parents waited patiently in the main cavern. Each cavern had different types of crystals and gems stuck to the walls. Small sea creatures clung to the walls and there were plants and corals growing from everywhere. Sammi Jo was sure that no one had ever seen these types of plants and corals before.

Eventually, she patted Screech on the back and pointed up. He took her back to the main cavern, and she thanked both of his parents for their hospitality and said that she would have to get home before her parents started to worry.

Sammi Jo held tightly onto Screech's back as they swam swiftly back to the beach where they had met.

"Thank you so much!" she exclaimed as he dropped her off at the shore. "I could never imagine a world like that. It's so quiet and beautiful!"

"Do you want to see more?" asked Screech.

"Oh, yes!" said Sammi Jo, "Will you take me again?"

"There is no end to the things I can show you," said Screech. "Do you want to see the seahorses tomorrow?"

"Absolutely! I will see you in the morning!" she said as she waved good-bye and started back up the beach toward home.

She ran up the stairs of her house and burst through the back door.

"Mom! Dad! Wait until you hear about my day!

This was *Absolute, positively the best day ever*!"

Dear Kara,

You absolutely need to find the time to come and visit me. I had the most incredible adventure today and there are so many more to come!

Screech took me in the ocean and we went to his home to meet his parents. I saw millions of beautiful sea creatures and rocks and plants and corals and his dad gave me a rock that glows and is stuck all over the walls of their cave. I could never describe to you how wonderful it all was. But, I sure hope I can show you sometime soon.

Tomorrow, he is taking me to meet seahorses. He says that these seahorses are something different than anything any human has ever seen before. I can't wait!

Please try to come and see me sometime soon so I can share all of these wonderful adventures with you!

Love,
Sammi Jo